Steven M. F. Cohen

BIRDIES, BIRDIES

Illustrated by
Olha Maksymtsiv

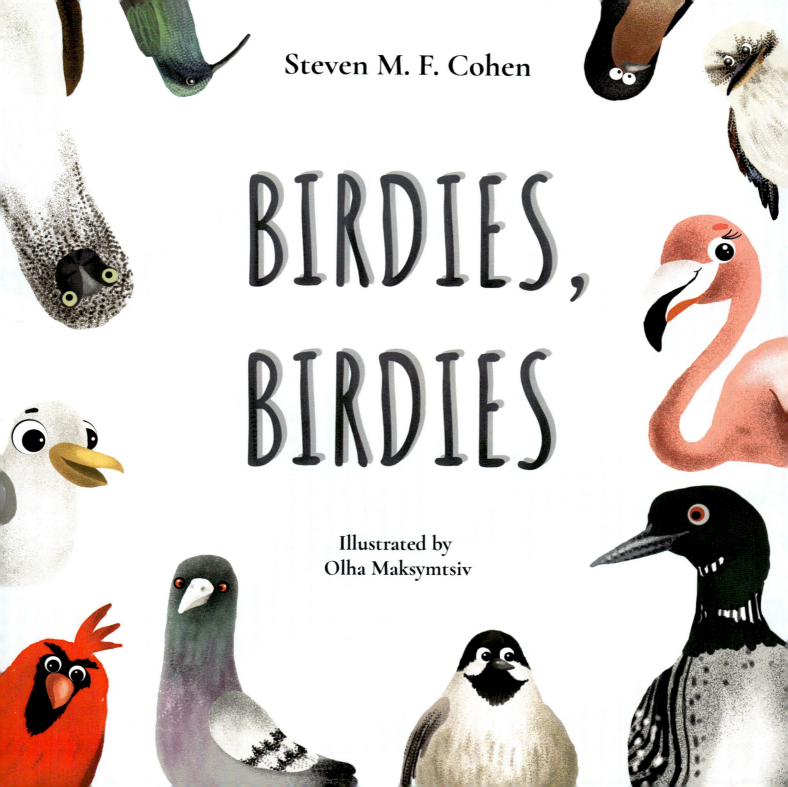

Steven M.F. Cohen could be reached at
smfcohen@gmail.com.

To order additional copies of this book, contact:
Xlibris
844-714-8691
www.Xlibris.com
Orders@Xlibris.com

ISBN: Softcover   978-1-6698-1548-8
       EBook   978-1-6698-1547-1

Print information available on the last page

Rev. date: 03/15/2022

For the children of Ukraine

May peace, freedom, awareness, the arts, nature, wonder, love
and joy fill all the days of your most precious lives.

*A portion of the proceeds will go to children affected by war.

Birdies, birdies in the sky
Birdies, birdies way up high
Birdies, birdies in the air
Birdies, birdies everywhere

Like the clouds they gently float
All covered in a feathered coat
Wings of color, wings so strong
Some birds fly the whole day long

4

DO YOU KNOW
THE NAMES OF THE BIRDS
IN THE PICTURE?
LET'S FIND OUT TOGETHER!

Some fly by night, some fly by day
Some birds migrate, some birds stay
Birdies, birdies in the tree
So many birds let's look and see

6

Blue Jays make a cawing sound
Their little chicks fall to the ground
Don't pick them up as you walk by
Up to a branch they soon will fly

Chickadees go, "Chick-a-dee-dee-dee"
Chirping their song so joyfully
They are brown, and black and white
On tiny twigs they hold tight

Cardinals are crimson red
They wear a crest upon their head
So easily they can be seen
Next to the leaves so very green

12

Peacocks strut their brilliant tails
Of course these are the show-off males
They spread them wide to find a mate
Majestic are their calls so great

Why are pink flamingos pink?
It has something to do with shrimp I think
They love to stand upon one leg
But cannot do this when they sit on an egg

Over the water pelicans skim
Scooping up fish as they swim
They carry them inside their bill
Gobb'ling them up 'til they have their fill

Owls hoot and owls holler
Turning their heads within a collar
At night they open up their eyes
And look into the starlit skies

19

Barn swallows flutter from rafters to beams
They move like bats or so it seems
But they're so very different creatures
Especially in their unique features

Seagulls glide over the sea
Catching the wind, ever so free
They like to gather on the beach
You may get close within their reach

24

The mockingbird sings an endless song
Mimicking bird songs all day long
Amazing virtuosity
Operatic and so witty

Penguins swim in the ocean
Hardly making any motion
Most live in earth's coldest places
We all love their cutest faces

Mourning doves coo, they do not tweet
Spinning out notes so very sweet
In the morning there's a chorus
A symphony is playing for us

Red breasted robins welcome in the spring
"The winter is over!", that's what they sing
Bye bye winter, bye bye snow
The robins are here, it's time for you to go

Parrots speak some awesome words
You must admit they are fun birds
We enjoy making them talk
They trod so slowly when they walk

Eagles can nest on a mountain side
Then glide in circles extremely wide
Bald and Golden, noble flyer
Soaring higher, higher, higher

With tiny wings the hummingbird
Speedily flaps yet can't be heard
Into a flower it sticks its long beak
Always playing hide and seek

Swans ever so white slide over the lake
So very silent, no sound do they make
A water ballet, a pas de deux
Gracefully dancing two by two

Duckies waddle and quack, quack, quack
No water rests upon their back
You can feed them bread,
     you can feed them crackers
Again I say they are great quackers

Chickens cluck and rooster crow
"Cock-a-doodle-doo" they go
White chickens lay white eggs,
                brown chickens lay brown
Upon their heads crests look like a crown

A homing pigeon can fly away
Then fly back home another day
Unbelievable directions
They never have to make corrections

Oh glorious bird of peace and love
Our world's most precious gift, the dove
Gentle spirit, beauty, grace
May our joyous souls embrace

Look! A bird with blue feet!
Isn't that neat?
It's a blue-footed booby from Galapagos Isle
Look! You can spot it a mile!

Whip-poor-will, whip-poor-will,
       whip-poor-will, whip-poor-will
Repeats its name while perching still
Whip-poor-will, whip-poor-will,
       whip-poor-will, whip-poor-will
A nocturnal call, a musical trill

Kookaburra laughs, all day long
Sitting in a gum tree laughs a laughing song
Belly belly laughter comes so deep within
Kookaburra laughs with a silly silly grin

54

The bird-of-paradise puts
on extravagant courting displays
A full spectrum of bright plumage;
brilliant color arrays
His well choreographed dance
is so marvelously done
It's as miraculous as the planets,
all circling the sun

Two-toed ostrich, largest bird of all
Flightless fowl 'round 9 feet tall
Go ahead, stick your head
in the ground
And turn your enormous eggs
round and round

From pole to pole fly the arctic terns
Through the frigid skies
        to their home nest returns
Longest journey on earth
        this marathoner makes
Migrating millions of miles
        over oceans and lakes

Hawks are birds of prey that eat
small critters like mice
Some think that isn't very nice
Raptors is their special name
It is quite hard to make them tame

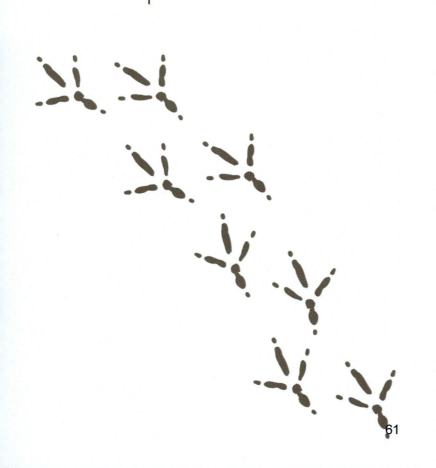

There is a land where
                    the partridge drums
A sacred land from which it comes
It beats its wings upon the land
And plays the drum with a sacred hand

The most haunting of cries is the wail
of the loon
On the lake it slides through the light
of the moon
With its dagger-like bill it fishes all day
By diving deep, then glissades away

And thus, the albatross does coast
o're ships far out at sea
"Upon a painted ocean" this god-like bird
glides free
A sailor's delight, for good luck
does it bring
Longest wingspan of all, this great
bird is the king

A snare is placed around its throat
Big fish are spit into the boat
This is quite an ingenious technique
Cormorant fishing, ancient and unique

You'd think by now that woodpecker
would have a headache!
But no, the pecking goes on and on
for goodness' sake!
All of this peck, peck, peck, peck, peck -
just for a little bug!
To survive this racket I'll have to wrap
my head with a very large rug!

Wild turkeys roost on branches,
tame turkeys roost in pens
The male is called a tom, female turkeys
are called hens
Gobble, gobble side to side, gobble,
gobble to and fro
Their poop defines their gender,
that's so funny, don't y'know?

Pterodactyl-like
    for the modern day
The great blue heron flaps away
In marshes camouflaged will stand
Just like a soldier, tall and grand

My darling baby puffin
My puffling, sweetest muffin
Go swimmy in the chilly sea
Then straight back to your burrow
to mommy

Sparrow, sparrow, little sparrow
Flitter through flowers, daisies and yarrow
Sparrows are found around the planet
Flying through cities of steel and granite

There is something you must know
The raven isn't a large crow
Both are glossy and black,
 but here's where it ends
Cawing crows and gronking ravens
 are not even friends

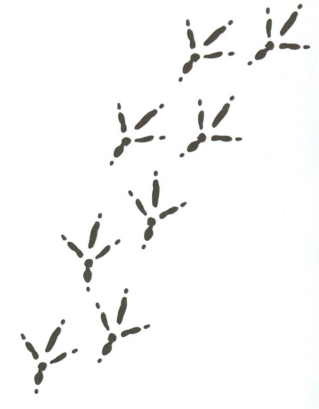

The cutest name is the tufted titmouse
Inside woodpecker holes it builds its house
Making nests with hair
                                    from every kind of critter
Eating wasps,snails and spiders
                                                    must be bitter

The fastest animal species alive
The peregrine falcon stoops and dives
Stunning its prey 200 miles per hour
and more

Aerodynamically, it soars!

I had a parakeet so green
It preened itself, it was so clean
I fed it tiny little seeds
And took care of all its needs

I also had a little finch
And when I held it, it's claws pinched
But still I held it all day long
And listened to its lovely song

Baby birds nestle up in a nest
Mamas hardly take a rest
Placing worms into their beaks
Under her a baby peaks

As morning comes and the day breaks
Upon a branch a birdie wakes
And sings a melody so clear
That you can hear it far and near

94

Marvelous birds around the world
With wings extended and unfurled
Some fly alone, some fly in flocks
Some sit on rooftops, some on rocks

CHIRP

COCK-A-DOODLE-DO

I wish that I could be a bird
And live without saying a word
And have a language of my own
Making sounds with a brilliant tone

HOOT

QUACK

GOBBLE

HONK

CLUCK

TRANSLATION

BIRD'S LANGUAGE	HUMAN LANGUAGE
CHICK-A-DEE-DEE-DEE!	GOOD MORNING TO YOU!

I watch for them
        throughout the year
To me they are so very dear
Birdies, birdies in the air
Birdies, birdies everywhere

Printed in the United States
by Baker & Taylor Publisher Services